SCHUBERT

MOMENTS MUSICAUX, OP. 94
IMPROMPTUS, OPP. 90 & 142

FOR THE PIANO

EDITED BY MURRAY BAYLOR

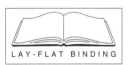

Alfred has made every effort to make this book not only attractive but more useful and long-lasting as well. Usually, large books do not lie flat or stay open on the music rack. In addition, the pages (which are glued together) tend to break away from the spine after repeated use.

In this edition, pages are sewn together in multiples of 16. This special process prevents pages from falling out of the book while allowing it to stay open for ease in playing. We hope this unique binding will give you added pleasure and additional use.

Third Edition

Cover art: Schubert at the Piano, *1899*
  by Gustav Klimt (Austrian, 1862–1918)
  Reproduction of original destroyed during World War II
  Erich Lessing/Art Resource, New York

CONTENTS

FOREWORD

FRANZ SCHUBERT
(1797–1828)

Of the many famous composers who lived and worked in Vienna, Europe's most musical city, Franz Schubert was the only one who made his home there from birth to death. Though his genius was recognized by a few when he was a child—and he had written at least one great masterpiece by the time he was seventeen—only a small part of his music had been published when he died at the age of 31. Considering the fact that he had had little more than a dozen years as a mature composer, the large, rich heritage of wonderful vocal and instrumental music that he produced is indeed astonishing.

SCHUBERT'S PIANO MUSIC

Schubert's music seems to fall between classical and romantic classifications—perhaps between that of Beethoven and Chopin. Although he first became known in Vienna as a composer of *lieder*, the piano was his instrument, and he wrote some of his finest music for piano solo and piano duet. The kind of instrument he played, however, usually called a fortepiano, was very different from a modern Steinway. In the *Kunsthistorische Museum* in Vienna there is a well-maintained piano that he once owned.

Its compass is from the F an octave below the bass staff to the F two octaves above the treble—six octaves in all. The action is light and the key drop shallow, permitting brisk tempos. It is a piano, of course, for a home, not a concert hall. While the volume is small compared with a modern instrument and the sound decay is short, the tone is bright, silvery and attractive, particularly in the upper octaves.

Because of these limiting characteristics, the music that Schubert wrote for this kind of instrument was quite different from that written by later composers. His music, on the whole, was not intended for a virtuoso playing in a concert hall but for the musician communicating with friends in more intimate surroundings. Probably because of his love of singing and song writing, he often incorporated in his piano music singable melodies that must be phrased with the breath pauses and points of emphasis that a fine singer would give to a song. Not only the spirit of song pervades this music, but also the spirit of dance. In the Vienna of his time, social dancing was very popular among young people, and Schubert often played for his friends to dance. Out of these improvisations he wrote about 400 short waltzes, écossaises, minuets, ländler, galops, etc.

In addition to his melodic gift, another part of the originality of Schubert's music lies in his use of harmony—his subtle or bold modulations, often to the mediant or the submediant, his use of the Neapolitan chord, his unexpected, poignant shifts from major to minor, and his expressive use of dissonance; all are used in a very personal way. Repeated chords, frequently with quick left-hand jumps, are characteristic. In triple meter, Schubert may briefly contradict the rhythmic pulse by accenting every other beat, thus giving the impression of a change to duple meter—a hemiola—measures that a 20th-century composer might notate as a change from 3/4 to 2/4 time.

Another unusual rhythmic aspect of Schubert's music is his ambiguous use of the dotted-eighth, sixteenth figure. Sometimes he used it in a literal sense, but at other times he often used it to indicate a rhythm with a dot of variable length as used by baroque composers (and some of today's popular-music performers). When he wrote:

to sound simultaneously with eighth-note triplets in another voice, it was usually intended to sound like:

conforming to the triplet rhythm:

Playing the sixteenth note after the triplet, as one might if interpreting it literally, usually sounds clumsy, although exceptions do occur, and so it will be seen quickly that this rule of the "variable dot" doesn't apply to all situations.

Other ambiguities in the interpretation of Schubert's music occur in his use of common ornaments. Most often single grace notes are melodic ornaments played before the beat, though there are exceptions, when harmonic ornaments—appoggiaturas on the beat—were probably intended. Pairs of grace notes or groups of three are also normally played before the beat as melodic ornaments. Trills start on the main note rather than on the auxiliary, and the *Pralltriller*—the short trill or inverted mordent (♆)—is played as a three-note figure. For turns, however, classical practice should be followed, namely, over the note:

and turns between notes:

Finally, a word concerning opus numbers. Unfortunately, the opus numbers for Schubert's music were assigned in chaotic order by publishers, most of them after his death. Opus 94, for instance, was written before opus 90. Accordingly, the most reliable guide to the chronological order of the compositions are the numbers assigned by Otto Erich Deutsch in his thematic catalogue (for example, D. 935 to represent op. 142) and they are frequently used to identify the works, in addition to, or as a substitute for, the opus numbers.

THIS EDITION

This edition has been prepared using photoduplicates and microfilm copies of Schubert's manuscripts of both sets of the impromptus, graciously provided by the Pierpont Morgan Library of New York City. The manuscript of the *Moments Musicaux* is lost; therefore the sources closest to the original for this set of pieces are the first complete edition published by Leidesdorf of Vienna in 1827, and the previously published numbers 3 and 6, all of which were furnished in microfilm copies by the British Library of London. We are also indebted to the scholarship of the late Christa Landon and Walther Durr whose admirable work for the fifth volume of the *Neue Schubert-Ausgabe: Werke für Klavier zu zwei Händen* (Bärenreiter-Verlag, 1984) has been helpful.

Fingerings, metronome marks in parentheses and pedalings are all editorial and should be understood to be only suggestions. Schubert's indications of pedaling are very rare and unspecific. The word *pedale* appears in the manuscript of the Impromptu, op. 90, no. 3 at the very beginning, and the words *con pedale* are to be found in his manuscript of the Impromptu op. 142, no. 1 under measure 69. These are the only indications of pedaling in the manuscripts of the Impromptus. Similarly, the first edition of the *Moments Musicaux* has only one pedal indication—in the fourth piece, on the second half of measure 21, and at the comparable place in the written out repeat. Considering the context and a number of obvious misprints in the first edition, this pedal indication seems to have been incorrectly positioned by the engraver. There is little doubt that Schubert used the pedal freely in his playing and intended its use in his music, though certainly not in the long washes of opaque sound that would be appropriate in the music of Liszt or Debussy.

Schubert's musical handwriting is clear in some respects, yet vague or unclear in others. There are revisions and emendations that probably indicate haste in copying. Slurs in the manuscript are not always clear as to where they start or end, and they are not always consistent. Accent marks (>) and diminuendo marks (⟩) are hard to distinguish from each other since they are often almost the same length. Dynamic indications are often sparse and inconsistent. There are places where ties from one measure to the next in sustained chords are not complete, and occasionally, intended accidentals have been omitted. In this edition accidentals not in the manuscript have been put in parentheses as well as a few editorial performance suggestions, which of course are not obligatory. One puzzling dynamic indication, *fp* ⟩ (see Impromptu, op. 90, no. 1, measure 196) is probably intended to mean *f* ⟩ *p*. Obvious oversights in slurring and ties have been corrected without comment.

6

THE MOMENTS MUSICAUX
Op. 94 (D. 780)

Since French was the second language of the sophisticated in Schubert's Vienna, these beautifully crafted vignettes were first published as a set in 1827 entitled, in the publisher's faulty French, *Momens Musicals*. The third of these had already been published in 1823 under the title *Air Russe* in an album of songs and piano pieces, and the sixth, under the title *Plaintes d'un Troubador*, had been published in 1824 in another album of mixed offerings. It is doubtful that these titles were Schubert's, though he may have agreed to the publisher's suggestions. It is still unclear whether or not he intended the six to appear as a set. Mendelssohn's later title, *Songs without Words*, might aptly apply to most of them. Though they are small-scale works, they are large in their range of beautiful emotional expression and artistic significance, and in their influence on later composers.

NO. 1 in C   *Page 13*

Paul Badura-Skoda has suggested that the first two measures of this piece, out of which the rest seems to grow, are like the sound of yodeling on a spring morning in the Austrian alps, and the added sound of a cuckoo (measures 18 and 19) further enhances this spring-time picture. Whether or not this was the inspiration, the piece is a delightful miniature. After the opening in C, the piece moves quickly through C minor, E-flat and G minor before returning to the home key (measure 8). After the repeat sign, the keys of A minor, G, and E minor are touched on, and a hemiola using accents and juxtaposed rhythmic figures occurs in measures 15 and 16. Returning to C, the opening material is presented in imitation between upper and lower voices (measures 22 through 24). Double counterpoint is used briefly in measures 26 through 29 (which inverts material from measures 5 through 8) to end the first section. The middle section introduces a triplet rhythm as the key of the dominant is established, and this motion of triplets is continued, supporting the melody (measure 38). The harmony now moves to D, the dominant, with another excursion into changed meter in measures 42 and 43. After G minor is introduced at measure 51, there is a return to the major to end the section. An 8-measure transition over a dominant pedal point leads back to the reprise of the first section.

NO. 2 in A-FLAT   *Page 16*

This lyrical piece contrasts the keys of A-flat and F-sharp minor in five alternating sections, joined, with one exception, by enharmonic dominants. The initial atmosphere is that of a meditative nocturne with 4-measure phrases that cadence first to the tonic and then to the dominant. A varied repeat of the first four measures is followed by an extended phrase that cadences to the subdominant, D-flat, the enharmonic equivalent of C-sharp and dominant of the next section.

The first occurrence of F-sharp minor introduces this section, with its repeated-note melody, widely spaced bass accompaniment and a 6-measure phrase followed by an 8-measure phrase. Then, a 4-measure link cadences to the submediant which becomes, again, the dominant of the next section. The recurrence of A-flat begins this section, repeating the initial six measures of the piece, but moves into G-flat before returning to the tonic. At measure 47 the E-flat in the bass clef, reiterated and extended through four measures, is like a distant horn call soon answered two octaves higher. A return to F-sharp minor without transition in measure 56 comes as an abrupt, dramatic surprise through the use of full chords for six measures. However, the succeeding measures return to the mood of the initial F-sharp minor section, with cadences to A and to F-sharp major before reaching another cadence to the submediant. The fifth and final section reviews, with only one new variant, material already heard.

Students who find the rhythm of the A-flat sections difficult to play accurately may find it easier to project the written rhythm against an imaginary background of steady eighth-note triplets in 3/4 time:

Careful balancing of the melody and the underlying chords will prevent an impression of heaviness in the A-flat sections.

NO. 3 in F MINOR   *Page 20*

This piece could be the music for a sprightly ballet with some kind of stamping, perhaps, as the right hand plays its accented quarter notes. Though it is the best known of all these pieces, it is not easy to play well because of difficulty in controlling the dynamics. The only loud portion of the piece arrives at measures 19 through 22, after which the indications are *p*, *pp*, *ppp*, *diminuendo*, and another *diminuendo*. This would seem to imply that a mere whisper should end the piece. After two measures of pizzicato-like introduction, the following 8-measure phrases (consisting of 2-measure motives) are clear and straightforward. The key centers are equally so—cadences change from F minor to A-flat and back again. Starting at measure 35, the comparatively long coda contrasts minor with major, and 6-measure phrases with 4-measure phrases, ending the piece in F major after playful harmonic twists.

NO. 4 in C-SHARP MINOR   *Page 22*

This piece, which looks like a Bach invention but sounds very different, begins as a kind of perpetual motion in sixteenth notes for the right hand. A legato right hand and a staccato left are propelled forward with unflagging energy. An 8-measure phrase and a 9-measure phrase move to the relative major of E, whereupon a 4-measure phrase leads to a kind of codetta of another 9 measures beginning at measure 22. The second part of this first section starts with the right hand duplicating the opening of the piece (measure 31), but a new, more melodic left-hand part is added. After a vigorous eight measures, a *pianissimo* (measure 39) begins similar 9-measure and 4-measure phrases which, this time, remain in the tonic key as they approach the codetta (measure 52). This codetta is similar to that of measures 22 through 30, though it remains in C-sharp minor. An implied dominant chord and a lengthened silent measure leads to the middle section.

In sharp contrast, the mood of this middle section is that of a merry folk dance in the parallel major (notated in D-flat). The third 4-measure phrase of this section goes to the unlikely key of F-flat, then these 12 measures are repeated. The following portion of the middle section continues in the same key with the same phrase structure until measures 84 and 85, when a return to D-flat is effected. The remainder of this section repeats material heard before, though now in the tonic. After repetition of the entire opening section and another surprise measure of lengthened silence, a whispered 4-measure coda juxtaposes the major and minor modes, ending the piece in C-sharp minor.

NO. 5 in F MINOR   *Page 26*

This piece is one of dark, violent expression. The basic figure of a quarter note and two eighths in each measure continues vigorously to measure 15 where the key changes to D-flat. The accented quarter notes and bass octaves sound threateningly, before a quick cadence to the dominant at the repeat sign. At measure 22 the original rhythmic figure continues with two measures in F minor and two in D-flat, the latter two echoed by a soft repeat. The next six measures repeat this unit a fourth higher in B-flat minor and G-flat. A new 6-measure unit appears (measure 34) with continuous right-hand eighth-note motion in B minor, followed in turn by a unit of similar length in C minor. Another 6-measure group starting at measure 46 introduces a new melodic pattern in A-flat minor and C-flat; then this is followed by a similar unit in A minor and C. A long transitional passage (4 + 4 + 2 + 8 measures) marks a return to the beginning of the piece with a literal repetition of eight measures. Although there is a shift in harmonic direction at measure 84, it first begins in the tonic key, moves to G-flat (measure 90), and the following passage duplicates measures 15 through 20 a fourth higher. This passage is succeeded by another quick cadence to F. The coda beginning at measure 97 in the tonic major, leads the piece to a cheerful ending.

This is the most difficult piece of the set. The phrase and key structure which are not easy to see must be understood before it can be learned efficiently and performed with confidence. To conquer its difficulties, first practice with pauses between phrase units and proceed with continuous practice in a rhythm that pauses on first beats—

$$\frac{3}{4} \; \quad \text{etc.}$$

—to secure hand placements. This will be found to be more effective than slow practice in the written rhythm of Schubert's original notation.

NO. 6 in A-FLAT   *Page 29*

Ostensibly, this is a minuet with trio—the kind that many composers before and after Schubert's time were writing, but there are enormous differences. Though the initial phrases are the 4- or 8-measure lengths of a dance, the powerful emotional expression, the subtle imbalance of the phrases, and the very original harmony are anything but conventional. The piece opens with a beautifully poised 8-measure phrase ending with a dominant cadence, then another phrase with a tonic cadence. The entire section is repeated.

A developmental section begins with an 8-measure phrase which cadences to the dominant of the tonic minor. The following nine-measure phrase, however, moves unexpectedly to the key of E followed by two 3-measure extensions confirming the new key. The next thirteen measures move the harmony by enharmonic chords back to a dominant six-five at measure 53, leading to an apparent reprise of the beginning. The following eight measures differ from the opening of the piece only in one small detail: the up-stemmed and dotted A-flat for the left hand in measure 57. (Was the discrepancy between this and the similar place in measure 4 an oversight on Schubert's part?) The following phrase of nine measures begins (at measure 62) with a repeated 2-measure motif, moves to a dramatic outburst notated in E, but arrives at the dominant of A-flat. This developmental section concludes with seven measures in the lower register that connote a hushed A-flat minor, cadencing to bare octaves.

The trio in the subdominant key moves serenely with two 4-measure phrases repeated in a higher octave. Similar 4-measure groups continue until measure 98 when a 6-measure phrase leads back to a repetition of the trio's opening. The 12 following measures end the section in the higher register.

While this piece doesn't have the technical hurdles found in the fourth or fifth pieces of the set, careful balancing of the often thickly written chords is necessary to avoid a ponderous effect and achieve one of richness and grace. It is also important for students to be aware of the striking suspensions and appoggiaturas that propel this remarkable harmony forward, a harmony of touching emotional effect.

IMPROMPTUS
OP. 90 (D. 899)

NO. 1 in C MINOR   *Page 32*

This highly original and characteristically Schubertian piece is a set of variations on two themes, one in the minor and the other in the major. After the dominant is sounded boldly in bare octaves, the first theme begins like a distant march with 4-measure phrases which cadence alternately to the dominant and the tonic. Unharmonized phrases implying dominant cadences are contrasted with harmonized phrases cadencing to the tonic. The last group of phrases, starting at measure 18, have ornamented melodic lines and chromatic harmony for the first phrases and vigorous bass octaves for the answering phrases. An 8-measure codetta begins at measure 33. The first theme, in its last echoing measures, gives way to an A-flat modulation, introducing the second theme with its triplet accompaniment. This theme glides forward in 5-measure phrases—and one of four measures—in the keys of A-flat and C-flat, then a variation on this theme begins (measure 60). A little codetta (measures 74 through 82) with poignant suspensions in the turn figure arising from the end of the theme, moves toward a 5-measure transitional passage which returns to C minor for a variation on the first theme. The march now begins in the bass, and a codetta to the variation (measures 111 to 119) leads to another transition (measures 120 to 124). A new variation (in G minor) on the second theme follows, with pizzicato-like bass accompaniment. Measure 152 marks the beginning of another delicate codetta to the second theme similar to measures 74 through 82, but now it is in the dominant. At measure 160, a final variation on the first theme alternates between major and minor in a way that Schubert has made so meaningful. A final coda with echo-like changes of register starts at measure 184 and recalls, in four of its measures, the opening octaves on the dominant.

Controversy arises in this piece over the question of how to properly play the dotted-eighth, sixteenth figure,

when there are simultaneous triplets in the accompaniment. Some performers play the figures to sound like:

as is usually the case in Schubert's compositions. Others, including this editor, feel it is more important to retain the march rhythm with crisp sixteenth notes throughout the piece, therefore playing the sixteenth note lightly *after* the last note of the triplet. More important than this technicality, however, is the necessity of projecting the dramatic changes (from sunny major to melancholy minor), the song-like melodies, the long lines of the phrases, and the subtle harmonic changes of this often unjustly neglected masterpiece.

NO. 2 in E-FLAT   *Page 43*

For most of its length, this popular piece achieves its unity—in part—by emphasizing the second beat of each measure. Although the right-hand line with its small upward leaps, downward diatonic scales and rising chromatic figures is clearly challenging, the part of the left hand with its varied ways of emphasizing the second beat deserves special attention and practice. The 8-measure phrases flow continuously in the tonic key until measure 25 when E-flat minor moves to A-flat minor. In every second measure the right hand adds emphasis to the second beat with half notes as the harmony moves downward to G-flat, F minor, and then back to E-flat minor. At measure 36 the harmonic motion stabilizes in G-flat, until the 8-measure dominant with a suspension (measure 44) leads to a return to the opening of the piece. With this reprise, however, there is only one 8-measure phrase in the middle register before a repeat in the higher register. Tension mounts as the rising chromatic figure extends to a climax on a high F while the bass moves downward through A-flat, G and F minor, arriving at E-flat minor. Measure 71 marks the beginning of four 3-measure phrases, during which a new *sforzando* emphasis is placed on the second beat (measure 77). This leads to a sweeping upward scale culminating on a powerful chord of G-flat, the enharmonic dominant of the following middle section.

Schubert's Piano

A new B-minor section progresses by 4-measure phrases and contrasting dynamics to F-sharp minor (measure 102), and back to a 2-measure phrase which negates the triple meter temporarily (measures 157 and 158). Then a six-four chord on E-flat, another two measures contradicting the meter, four measures of dominant, and a fermata on B-flat anticipate the *da capo*. The coda unifies the piece by contrasting the two principal key centers, swinging from B minor to E-flat (now minor) before the *accelerando*, which concludes the piece in exciting fashion. This is, incidentally, one of the rather few pieces in the piano repertory that begin in a major key and end in the tonic minor.

A good practice technique for the rippling right-hand passages is to mentally place a fermata over the first note of measures 1, 3, 5, 7, 9, etc. and then play from fermata to fermata in one sweep. This kind of rapid practice with pauses divides the problem into smaller steps which are easier to assimilate, and it helps concentration during performance.

NO. 3 in G-FLAT   Page 49

Carl Haslinger, who published this piece for the first time almost 30 years after Schubert's death evidently decided that the time signature (which had indicated 4/2 time) and the key signature might intimidate potential buyers; he had the piece transposed to G and changed to 4/4 time by cutting each measure in half with extra bar lines. Though this might have helped some readers, it actually made the playing more difficult and, since all the impromptus are in flat keys, spoiled the key relationships between the pieces if they were to be played as a group. Occasionally this changed version—with a few chords altered as well—is still published.

The elegant serenity of this piece is achieved by a spacious unfolding (in 4-measure phrases) of the song-like melody over the fluid sextuplet accompaniment. The middle section of the ternary form begins with a more active, dramatic bass line and less regular phrase lengths (measure 25). The key is now E-flat minor, moving to C-flat and back again before a return to the opening melody (measure 55). The last section of this ternary form begins with a literal reprise of the first section adding small variants at measure 63, but it takes a new turn toward the subdominant at measure 70. A coda starting at measure 74 brings the piece to a tranquil conclusion.

The playing problems are chiefly those of keeping the melody shaded and shaped against the bass line while maintaining the eighth notes as an unobtrusive background. At times a quick application of the soft pedal after a melody note is played can ease this difficulty.

NO. 4 in A-FLAT   Page 57

This impromptu, which begins with feathery descending figures in A-flat minor, moves in 6-measure phrases to C-flat and B minor before arriving at A-flat major, where new 4-measure phrases start (measure 31). At measure 47 a baritone melody enters under the hesitant phrases begun eight measures earlier. As the melody soars upward the tension increases while the harmony touches on B-flat minor and then comes to a climax on D-flat (measure 64). The descending sixteenth-note figures move toward a hemiola effect (measures 68 through 71) and the dominant sevenths (measures 70 and 71) which introduce related melodic material in triplets within the tonic key. Measures 80 to 95 are like measures 39 through 54, but the following nine measures remain in the tonic key rather than going to the subdominant as before. The dominant six-five (measures 105 and 106) by enharmonic equivalence, opens the door to the trio in C-sharp minor. Here throbbing repeated chords accompany a dramatic melody with regular phrase lengths but strong dynamic contrasts. At measure 123, 8-measure phrases sweep up and down like great waves until two delicate 4-measure phrases (measure 139) are followed by another powerful upward phrase of twelve measures. A 6-measure transition ends on a dominant seventh whose enharmonic equivalent is continued in the ensuing six measures. Then the re-established sixteenth-note motion prepares the way for a return to the beginning.

This piece is difficult to interpret because its elegance and grace are only apparent when it is played at a rapid enough tempo to maintain the long line of the phrases. Walter Gieseking played the right-hand sixteenths without using his thumb, saying that that was the best way to achieve perfect smoothness in these zigzag arpeggios. For most students a conventional fingering is more practical. Practicing the rhythm:

and blocking the chords by playing all the notes on one beat together in this manner:

are very helpful.

Schubert at the Piano
Detail from a watercolor by Kupelwieser

IMPROMPTUS
Op. 142 (D.935)

NO. 1 in F MINOR   Page 68

This impromptu is one of Schubert's most original creations so far as its form is concerned, and one of his most beautiful in its expression. The form has been described as a modified sonata-allegro (though the form here resembles none of Schubert's sonata movements), as a rondo, and as a hybrid of the two. Is it a unique form owing nothing to classical models? A thoughtful examination may reveal an answer. The work opens with an aggressive 4-measure flourish followed by a soft 2-measure reply. These six measures are repeated with embellishments before a fluttering right-hand theme is introduced (measure 13), predominantly in broken thirds and accompanied by light chords. As this first theme develops by 4-measure phrases and sequential passages, it modulates to A-flat for a second theme in octaves (measure 30) and then moves sequentially to F. A vigorous octave passage (measure 39) moves to A-flat to introduce a new lyric theme (measure 45) which progresses by 6-measure units. After a repetition of this theme played by the left hand, a transitional passage leads to new material. It is interesting that all the thematic material heard thus far is unified by a recurring pattern: three repeated pitches, a downward step, and the repetition of the three pitches. The top notes of the fluttering figure at measure 13, the octaves at measure 31, and the lyric theme at measure 45 all follow this pattern.

New material is introduced (measure 69) as the right hand starts a murmuring flow of sixteenth notes and the left hand crosses above and below to play both voices of a hushed dialogue. The key changes from A-flat minor to C-flat and back to A-flat minor (after the repeat sign), for an extension and development which eventually changes to A-flat major. Beginning at the second ending, six measures of transition lead to the second large section, in which all the elements heard thus far return in the tonic key. The proportional lengths within this section are almost identical to those of the first section. The opening twelve measures of the piece are repeated with small alterations (measure 115). The fluttering first theme recurs in F minor at measure 127, then continues in F major. The return of the second theme in octaves and its extensions starts at measure 144, and the lyrical third theme reappears—now in the major—at measure 159. The dialogued episode (measure 182) is in F minor moving to A-flat as it unfolds, and back to F. This dialogue continues in C briefly and, again, moves back to F before the coda. This coda modeled on the opening flourish ends the piece quietly.

This is one of the longest of the impromptus, and its chief difficulty is in the passages with hands crossing. Practicing each hand separately will help solve the problem. Other requirements for mastering this piece include sensitivity to melodic shapes and an awareness of the distinctive harmonies.

NO. 2 in A-FLAT   Page 83

This deservedly popular piece begins like a saraband in a gentle swaying rhythm. The first eight measures are repeated in a higher octave concluding with a turn embellishing the second cadence. The next fourteen measures—the middle section of this small ternary form—are more forceful and have two extra measures of dominant harmony to break the steady progress of 4-measure phrases before a return to the piece's opening material. At this point (measure 31), there appears a seemingly literal repetition of the beginning, but the second phrase introduces a G-flat in the bass (measure 35) making a small change in these 16 measures which balance with the opening section.

The trio contains rolling triplets with subtly changing harmonies in the subdominant key, contrasting with the first section of the piece. The opening 4 measures of the trio are repeated with the right hand an octave higher. A 4-measure extension concludes with a soft cadence; then the 12 measures are repeated. Following the repeat, a more melancholy expression begins in the key of D-flat minor, leading to a powerful climax in A major. Before the recapitulation of the first part of the trio begins, the bass trill in measure 76 sounds like a distant roll of thunder. A transition from measure 91 to 98 brings the listener back to a complete repetition of the opening of the piece, completed by a 4-measure coda.

The problem of playing the first and last parts is one of keeping the melody and bass line distinct from the remaining harmonic structure through dynamic contrast. Blocking the chords of the trio section by playing all three notes written on one beat as a chord, is an excellent practice technique for learning the hand positions and as an aid to memorization.

NO. 3 in B-FLAT   Page 88

The theme used for this set of variations is similar to one Schubert used as an *entr'acte* in *Rosamunde* as well as to one used in the *Andante* movement of his string quartet in A minor. The exquisite little theme—in two parts, each of 8 measures—cadences toward the tonic through a diminished-seventh chord in measure 7, to end the first half of this theme. The same chord appears in measure 14 of the theme's second half, after a small excursion away from the tonal center. A 2-measure codetta to the theme, repeating the final cadence, brings it to a graceful close. The first variation retains the basic harmony and phrase length of the theme but creates a new melody by weaving additional notes among those of the original melody. The second variation, again retaining the essential shape and harmony of the theme, adds a dainty right-hand melody to its first half and an assertive left-hand melody to the second. The third variation is an impassioned one. It departs further from the theme as the meter changes, the key changes to B-flat minor, and as the register is raised an octave for the literal repeat of the first half of this variation. The phrase lengths remain the same as those of the theme, but the second half takes a wider tonal orbit, moving to F before returning to the tonic and the expected codetta. The gloom of this variation is dispelled, however, by the perky fourth variation in G-flat with its arpeggiated melodies divided between hands. The codetta to this variation is extended to make a transition back to B-flat. The fifth and last variation is based on the second one. The original harmonic scheme with characteristic diminished seventh chords at the expected places reappears, and the glittering scale figures summon up the mood of a merry romp. The coda, extended to greater length, recalls the theme in a grave, meditative final statement that moves gently to the repose of the final cadence.

NO. 4 in F MINOR   Page 99

The last impromptu of this opus is the most brilliant, the least melodic, and the most difficult to interpret and play. It is a large-scale ternary form with a middle section in the relative major. The word *scherzando* indicates a joking, playful atmosphere, and the rhythmic figures suggest a lively Czech or Hungarian dance. The phrase lengths are regular through the first 16 measures and are not disturbed by the implied duple meter in measures 17 and 18, nor in 25 and 26. The nervous trills and the quick dashes up and down the keyboard over dissonant chords in the interlude (measures 36 through 44) suggest a shaken tambourine and the whirl of a dancer; then the dance rhythm resumes at measure 45. Though this appears to be a return to the beginning of the piece, a new departure at measure 59 takes the tonality further afield and uses more implied duple meter before arriving at a second interlude comparable to the one at measure 36.

The dominant seventh before the fermata (measure 86) opens the way to the second large section. More sparkling scale figures, alternating between A-flat major and A-flat minor, now appear in 8-measure groups. The *forte* in the last minor grouping precedes three 4-measure groups, ending at another fermata. A-flat minor is the tonality of the next section marked *con delicatezza*. These 4-measure groups, extended twice (measures 143 and 157), lead to a dominant pedal point and another measure of rest. Of a number of surprises which occur in this piece, the next is a change of key from A-flat to A over a dominant pedal point (measure 165) but measure 185 restores A-flat. This movement of a half step up and down recalls a similar motion in the first part of the piece at measures 30 through 35.

After five groups of four measures, scale passages in 8-measure groups rush up and down, changing from A-flat to A-flat minor and to A again before returning to A-flat (measure 231) and moving from A-flat to C. At measure 283 there begins a mysterious passage of irregular phrase lengths, chords suspended over muttering bass figures, and dramatic measures of extended silence. The last fermata is on a C chord, the dominant, followed by 12 measures of C major, which anticipate the recapitulation of the first section. A literal repetition of 85 measures takes place before a long coda begins (measure 420) with a bouncing right-hand part which continues in 8-measure groups over solemnly changing left-hand chords. After two silent measures, the *più presto* builds in power and tension over three 8-measure groups and one of four measures, before a final precipitous plunge covering six octaves down to the low F.

The difficulties of learning and playing this piece are those of controlling a fine and varied staccato, playing seamless, glittering scale passages, and establishing and maintaining the continuity that results from thinking in long sections that are the building stones of this remarkable music.

RECOMMENDED READING

Abraham, Gerald, editor, *The Music of Schubert*
(W. W. Norton, 1947).
Brown, Maurice J.E., *The New Grove Schubert*
(W. W. Norton, 1983).
Deutsch, Otto Erich, *The Schubert Reader*
(W. W. Norton, 1947).

Marek, George R., *Schubert*
(Viking-Penguin, 1985).
Osborne, Charles, *Schubert and his Vienna*
(Alfred A. Knopf, 1985).

RECOMMENDED LISTENING

All six *Moments Musicaux* have been recorded by Paul Badura-Skoda, Daniel Barenboim, Alfred Brendel, Rudolf Buchbinder, Clifford Curzon, Jörg Demus, Edwin Fischer, Peter Frankl, Emil Gilels, Friedrich Gulda, Walter Hautzig, Lee Luvisi, Vladimir Nilssen, Artur Schnabel and Karl Ulrich. They have also been recorded by Jörg Dahler and Paul Badura-Skoda on fortepianos made in Schubert's lifetime. Individual numbers from the set have been recorded by many other pianists.

Both sets of impromptus have been recorded by Augustin Anievas, Rudolf Buchbinder, Jörg Demus, Brigitte Engerer, Edwin Fischer, Peter Frankl, Walter Gieseking, Friedrich Gulda, Ingrid Haebler, Wilhelm Kempf, Radu Lupu, Murray Perahia and Artur Schnabel. The impromptus in op. 90 have been recorded by Carol Rosenberger and Claudio Arrau. Those in op. 142 have been recorded by Rudolf Serkin. Other artists have recorded individual impromptus from either or both sets.

ACKNOWLEDGMENTS

We are grateful to Dr. J. Rigbie Turner, curator of music manuscripts at the Pierpont Morgan Library, for providing us with copies of Schubert's manuscripts for all eight impromptus, and to the board of the British Library for allowing microfilms of the earliest publications of the *Moments Musicaux* to be made and sent. We owe thanks as well to a number of individuals who have been helpful in the preparation of this edition, among them Jeff Douglas and Irene Ponce who aided in obtaining library materials, Rose Hane who typed the written text, Creston Klingman and Ted Prochazcha who helped with the proofreading, Patrick Wilson who gave editorial assistance, and Elisabeth Baylor and Morton Manus whose encouragement and help were ever present.

A Schubertiade—Schubert is seated at the piano with the singer Vogl beside him.
From a painting by Moritz von Schwind.

MOMENTS MUSICAUX

Opus 94 · D. 780

(a) The grace notes in the first measure and in all similar rhythmic figures are played before the beat.

(b) In measures 30 and 31, and in measures 51 and 52 as well, the highest sounding notes are often played like a melody emerging from the triplets in the rhythm ♩ ♩ ♩ | ♩ ♩ ♩ or ♩ ♩ ♩ | ♩ ♩.

(c) In measures 38 and 39 and those that follow, in accordance with rhythmic conventions often used by Schubert, the rhythm for the right hand is played ♩ ♪₃♪ | ♪₃♪ ♩ , the sixteenth note coinciding with the third note of the left hand triplet.

(a) The grace notes in this piece are all played before the beat except for measures 16 and 81.

(b) The grace notes on the second and third beats of this measure, and measure 81, are sometimes played like the others in this piece, and sometimes as appoggiaturas on the beat, thus:

18

20

3.

Allegro moderato ($\quad$ = c.92)

(a) The grace notes are all played quickly, before the beat. The left-hand part of this piece, which suggests string pizzicato, has staccato marks for only the first two measures in all the sources, as given here. Staccato is implied for the remainder of the left-hand part, though this need not be taken literally, playing the whole piece without pedal.

21

4.

Moderato (♩ = c.108)

p legato

staccato

⒜ This measure and measure 123 in the source (the *da capo*) have the only pedal indications in this set of pieces, evidently misplaced by the engraver, on the second beat of the measure.

23

ⓑ The slurring for this section is inconsistent in the first edition. Should it be 𝄽𝅘𝅥𝅮 or 𝄽𝅘𝅥𝅮 ?

ⓒ If Schubert's accent marks in measures 62 through 101 are not treated carefully, the listener will have the impression that the rhythm is 𝄽𝅘𝅥𝅮 , etc. Of course this would disrupt the scanning and result in a bad connection with the first and last sections. In measure 62 particularly, it is necessary by rhythmic nuance and pedaling to make clear where the first beat of the measure falls.

ⓓ There is confusion in the first and subsequent editions about the first treble clef note in measures 78 and 80. It should almost certainly be F-natural as given here.

Allegro vivace (♩ = c.116)

5.

(a) In measures 5 through 8, the melody is in the lower notes of the treble clef.

(b) There is the possibility that the repeat from measure 22 should begin after measure 96 rather than after the last measure. If this is the case, measures 97 through 110 would become a coda. From a musical standpoint this would be quite convincing, though most editions give the repeat as indicated here.

Allegretto (♩ = c.116)

6.

ⓐ The grace note sounds best played before the beat.

ⓑ In measures 35 and 38, the pairs of grace notes may be played before the beat or as appoggiaturas on the beat, thus:

30

ⓒ Measures 51 to 56: The first complete edition and the "Plaintes d'un Troubadour" in the *Album Musical* do not agree on minor details for this piece.   The version given here seems the most acceptable of several choices.

ⓓ The grace note is played before the beat.

IMPROMPTUS

Opus 90 · D. 899

Allegro molto moderato (♩ = c.88-100)

ⓐ The grace notes might be played before the beat, or perhaps better, on the beat, thus:

ⓑ The trill on the last beat is usually played:

(c) The grace notes are played as acciaccaturas, quickly, before the beat.

(d) The grace notes are played before the beat.

(e) Measures 41, 46, and similar figures: The fourth beat in the right hand might be played ♩♪ —the last note coinciding with the last note of the accompanying triplet figure in the left hand—or, if the player prefers to maintain a strong march rhythm, as a modern dotted eighth-sixteenth note, the sixteenth lightly following the last note of the triplet.

(f) In measures 41 through 60 (and in similar places), "finger pedaling"—holding down the first note of each triplet while playing the other two notes —is another possible solution to the pedaling problem.

(g) In measures 75 and 76, and in similar places, the grace notes are played either before the beat, or as appoggiaturas on the beat, thus:

(h) The grace note is probably best played as an appoggiature on the beat, thus:

ⓘ If the dotted eighth-sixteenth note figure has been played to coincide with the triplets, this rhythmically difficult passage may be played as in Example 1. If the sixteenth notes are being played precisely as sixteenths, play as in Example 2.

Example 1   Example 2

ⓙ The grace note should be played to agree with the one in measure 99.

(k) In this passage the bass line is played like cello pizzicato, against the singing melody in the soprano and the delicate accompanying figure in the middle of the texture.

① Staccato articulation was the probable intention for the right hand through m. 148.

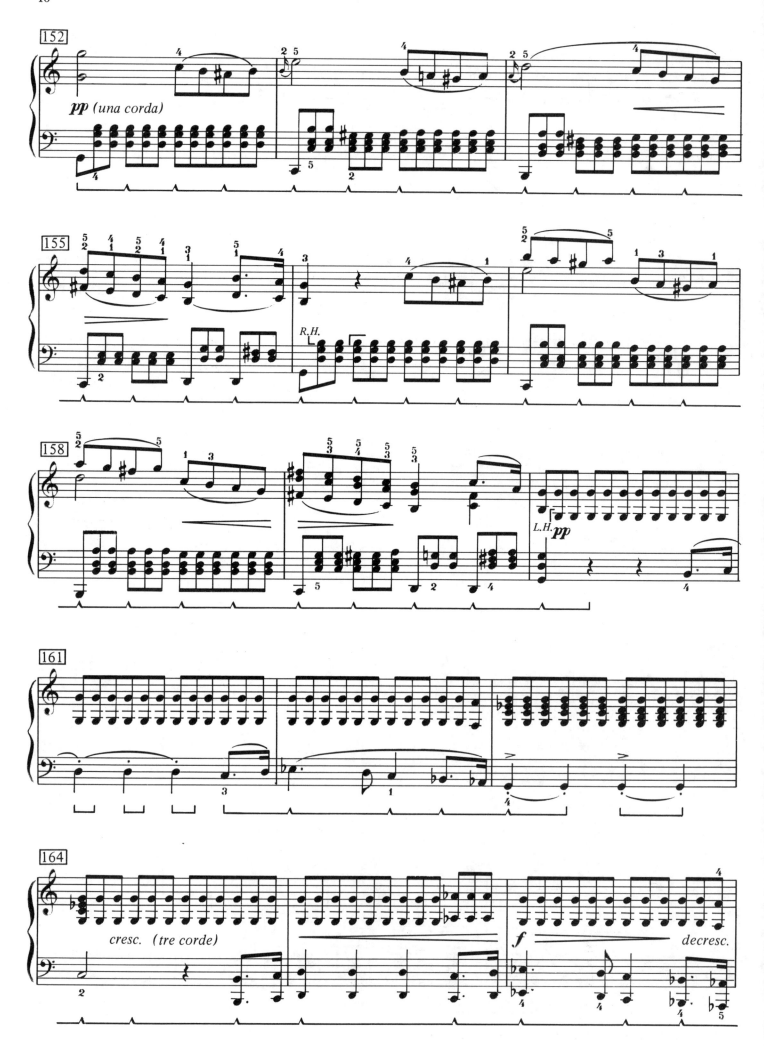

Ⓜ The solution to the rhythmic problem here is similar to that of measure 105.

(a) In measures 2, 10, and similar places, the parenthesized quarter rests are editorial. Schubert, probably writing in haste, evidently overlooked the fact that what he'd written, taken literally, was impossible.

46

ⓑ In measures 90-92, the last note, r.h. is inconsistent in the ms with respect to length of the note.

Da Capo al Segno e poi la Coda

48

ⓐ The long jump in the bass clef on the third beat of the measure may be played as indicated above, treating the F like a grace note before the right hand A-flat, or it may be played   catching the low D-flat with the damper pedal.

ⓑ This interval, in measures 5 and 59, was changed in the first transposed edition to F and D-natural, with a corresponding D-natural in the right hand.   The ms has only the notes given here.

50

© The editorial F-flats are not in Schubert's manuscript and must have been an oversight in quick writing. F-naturals sound crude, and measures 19 and 65, which are similar, have F-flats in the manuscript.

ⓓ The trill for the left hand at the end of the measure may be played thus:

ⓔ The left-hand trill on the last beat of the measure may be played thus:

52

(f) The left-hand trill on the second beat of the measure may be played:

(g) Here Schubert might have added the sub-octave to the F and the three following bass notes, but his piano didn't go below the low F.   Should these notes be added?

(h) The parenthesized natural for the C on the fifth quarter-note beat is editorial. In the manuscript the natural sign is found only on the seventh quarter-note beat. Again, this was probably an omission due to hasty writing.

ⓘ The left hand trill on the second half of the measure may be played:

ⓙ The manuscript has a long flat fermata sign both above and below the last six eighth notes of this measure, apparently meant to indicate a ritard toward the last note of the measure, and a pause before continuing.

(k) The left-hand trill is played like that in measure 19.

Ⓣ The left-hand trill is played thus:

Ⓜ The left-hand trill follows the pattern of the one in measure 53.

(a) In measures 2, 4, 8, etc., the editorial eighth rest is added because the left hand must release a key so that it can be played by the right hand.

(b) The last chord for the left hand is not marked staccato in the manuscript, though it can be assumed that this was the intention in this and similar places.

(c) In measures 2, 4, 8, 10, etc., ties for chords sustained into these measures by the left hand are not completely written out in the manuscript, though the intention is again clear. Repeated slurs and accent marks are often missing as well.

58

Trio (♩ = c.126)
tension, excitement

62

63

ⓓ There is the possibility that Schubert intended, but forgot to write ties from measure 168 to 169 in the bass clef.
Most editions show the chord reiterated as given here.

IMPROMPTUS

Opus 142 · D. 935

ⓐ The three grace notes sound best played as a triplet before the rolled left-hand chord.

ⓑ The grace notes are played before the beat in measures 4 and 10.

ⓒ Of several possible ways of playing the turns in measures 7 and 8, without slowing the tempo, the most satisfactory might be:

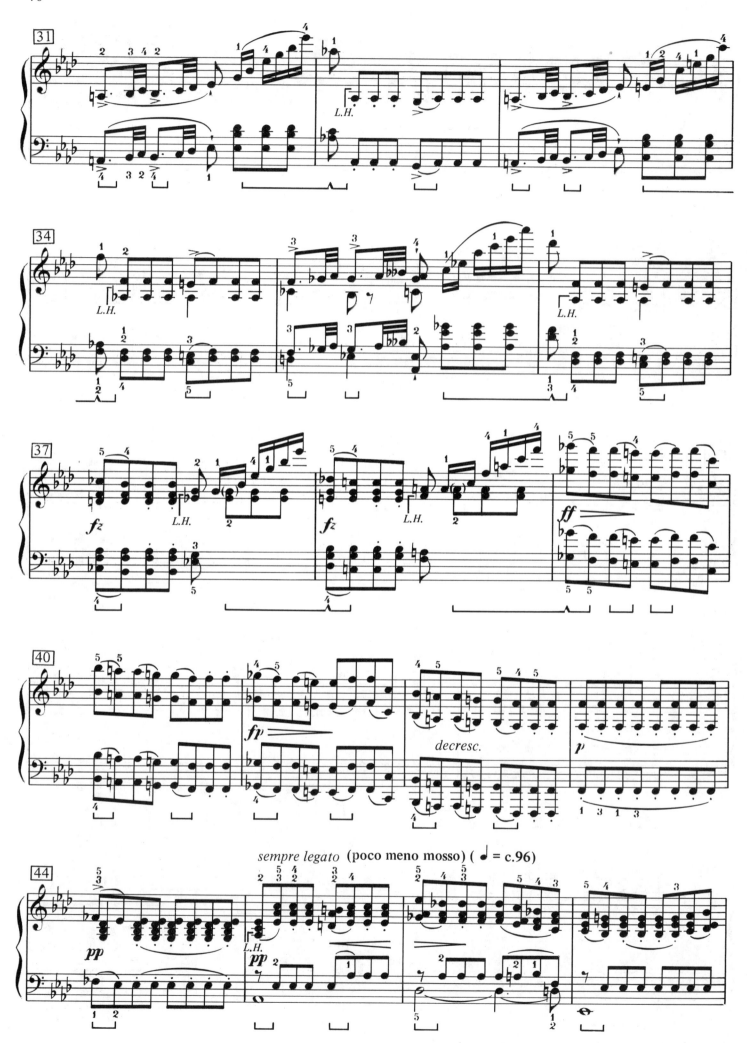

sempre legato (poco meno mosso) (♩ = c.96)

ⓓ The grace notes are best played before the beat in measures 48, 54, 60, and 62.

72

(e) Below the first measure of this section in the manuscript are the words "con pedale," one of Schubert's rare indications that the pedal is to be used.

(f) The return repeat sign was inadvertently omitted in the manuscript, and the original publisher, misunderstanding, omitted the repeated section from measure 84 through 109a.

74

(g) In measures 115, 118, 121, and 124, the grace notes are played as in the first part of the piece.

(h) In measure 162 and similar places, the grace notes are played before the beat, as in the first part of the piece.

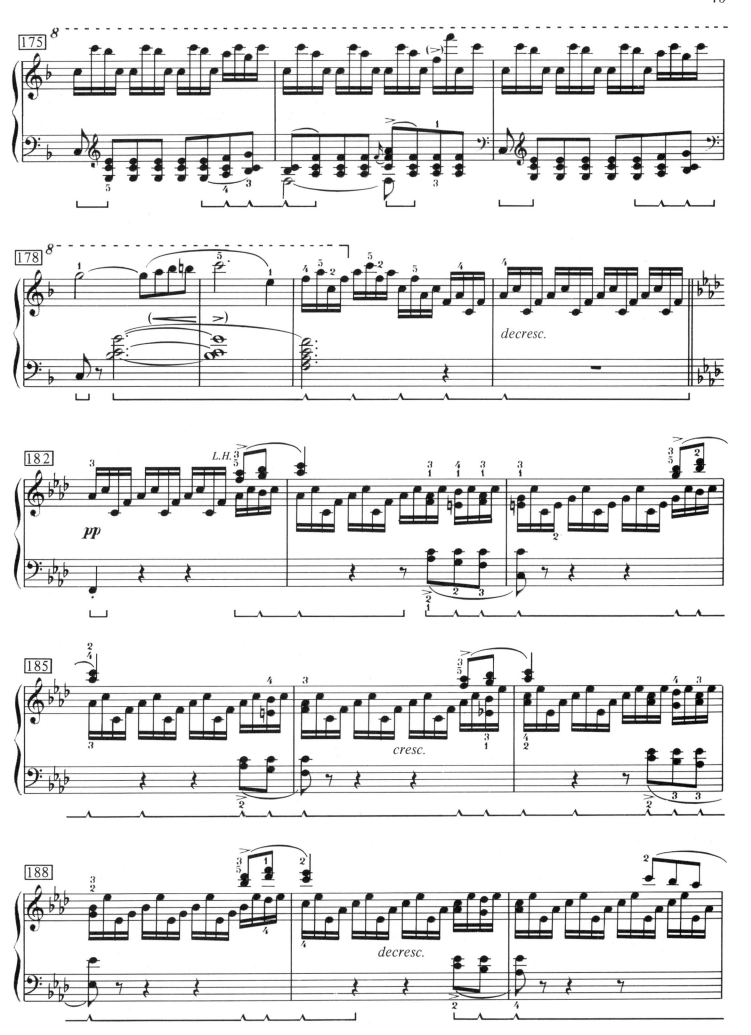

(i) The turns should agree with those played in the first part of the piece.

ⓐ The turn may be played: or

ⓑ The rhythm of measures 27 and 28 could be: or

ⓒ The manuscript has wide fermatas over and under the first two beats of measure 30, implying a ritard, a pause, and then a return to the original tempo on the third beat.

(d) Schubert might have written the bass-clef E's an octave lower in measure 68, but his piano had the F of the previous measure as its lowest note.

(e) The bass-clef trill may be played:

(f) In measures 113 and 125, the ornaments should agree with those played in the first part of the piece: measures 15, 27 and 28.

Thema

Andante (♩ = c.92)

3.

(a) The grace note is best played before the beat, thus:

(b) The pair of grace notes is also best played before the beat, thus:

(c) A graceful solution to the rhythmic problem of this measure might be:

poco rit.

Var. I (♩ = c.100)

Var. II (♩ = c.100)

ⓓ The turn in measures 38 and 42 is usually played:

ⓔ To keep a steady tempo the trill might be a short one, thus:

or, more elaborately:

(f) The pairs of grace notes sound best before the beat.

(g) In measures 52, 53 and 54, the grace notes should be acciaccaturas, played quickly with the following note.

(h) In measures 56, 57 and 58, and in the rest of the variation, the sixteenth notes following dotted eighths should coincide with the last eighth note of the left-hand triplet (see foreword).

(i) In measures 72 and 77, the grace notes are played before the beat.

Var. V (♪ = c.96)

98

(j) The figure with the trill under the *al 'ottava* sign might be played thus:

or with more reiterations of the trilled notes and a trill ending—perhaps a slight ritard as well—thus:

(a) The grace notes in measures 1, 2, 3 and similar passages, are quick acciaccaturas, though there is a possibility that the one in measure 3 should be an appoggiatura, so that measure 3 would sound like measures 47, 338, and 382.

(b) In measures 36, 38, 40, 42 and in similar places later in the piece, the trills begin on the principal note, not on the auxiliary.

(c) Schubert might have written measures 40, 41 and 42, as well as measures 81 to 83 and 416 to 418, to follow the more sweeping up-and-down pattern of measures 42 and 43 if his piano had had the range to go above the top F. Should we make such a substitution?

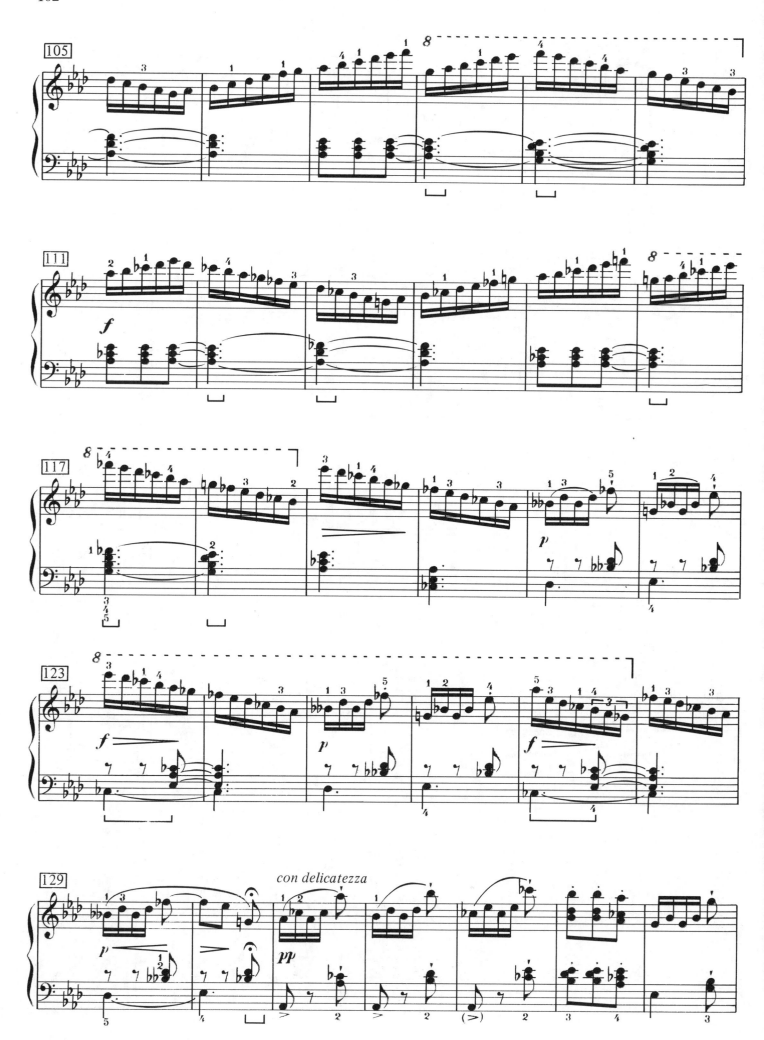

106

108

110

(d) The three grace notes are played before the beat.